D0185910

lauren child

My wobbly tooth must NOT ever NEVER fall out

PUFFIN

Charlie and Lola™

Text based on script written by Samantha Hill

Illustrations from the TV animation
produced by Tiger Aspect

PUFFIN BOOKS
Published by the Penguin Group: London, New York, Ireland, Australia,
Canada, India, New Zealand and South Africa
Penguin Books Ltd, Registered Offices: 80 Strand, London WC2R 0RL, England

www.penguin.com

First published 2006
1 3 5 7 9 10 8 6 4 2
Text and illustrations copyright © Lauren Child/Tiger Aspect Productions Limited, 2006
The Charlie and Lola logo is a trademark of Lauren Child
All rights reserved
The moral right of the author/illustrator has been asserted
Made and printed in China
ISBN-13: 978-0-141-38240-1
ISBN-10: 0-141-38240-6

I have this little sister Lola.
She is small and very funny.
This week she got her
first ever wobbly tooth.

Lola says,
   "I do not ever NEVER want
my wobbly tooth to fall out.
        I need it."

Marv says, "When I had my first wobbly tooth,
        I nearly swallowed it.
      Luckily I was eating a toffee...
              and my tooth got stuck in it!"

I say, "Once I headed a football
and my wobbly tooth just flew out
of my mouth!"

"But I do not ever NEVER
want my wobbly tooth
to fall out," says Lola.

Marv says, "Why not?"

"I just need to keep completely
        all my teeth," says Lola.

And I say, "Those are just your baby teeth
        and they are meant to
get wobbly and fall out.
Then you will get new teeth – and
        they are your grown-up ones."

"It's like mooses," says Marv. "Mooses' antlers
fall off and then they get new ones which are
better and stronger."

"But I am not a moose!
And I like my teeth completely
the way they are... wobbly," says Lola.

Later Lotta comes over to play with Lola.

"Hello everybody,
        hello Lola. Look!"

Lola says,
"What is it, Lotta? What is it?"
And Lotta says,
        "My wobbly tooth fell out!"

"What did you get?"
says Marv.

"What do you **mean**, what did you **get**?" says Lola.
And Lotta says,
"Well, the **tooth fairy** came and..."
"Who is the **tooth fairy**?!" says Lola.

"Well, the tooth fairy is the tooth fairy...
      I put my wobbly tooth under my pillow,
      and then in the middle of the night
the tooth fairy came and she swapped it
for a coin," says Lotta.
      "And in the morning
I bought this for
      the farm.
It's a
      chicken!"

Lola says,

"I didn't know there was a special fairy who gives you things when your teeth fall out! Why didn't somebody tell me this before? Nobody told me about the tooth fairy!

"My wobbly tooth must absolutely,
        completely come out! Now!"

Lotta says,
"What will you get with your
        tooth money? We need a
horse and a sheep... and a cow."

And Lola says,
        "I'm going to get
        a giraffe."

"Do you get giraffes on a farm?"
says Lotta.

And Lola says,
"Yes, you absolutely do, Lotta...

"... but how do I get my wobbly tooth to fall out?"

And Lotta says, "You have to keep wobbling it."

Lola says, "I think it's almost nearly
about to come out..."
And Lotta says,
"Just keep wobbling it."

Marv says,
"Do you want me to twist it?"
"No Marv!" says Lola. "Mum said
absolutely no twisting, not never!"
And I say, "Keep wobbling, Lola."

"I am **wobbling** it,"
she says, "but it's still
not coming **out**.

I don't think it's **ever**
going to **come out**."

Then she squeals,
"Aaagh! Charlie...

It's out!
My wobbly tooth
is completely out!
And now I can get my giraffe!"

Lotta says,
    "Remember to put it under your pillow.
      You must go to bed early,
         and you must fall asleep quickly,
  or the tooth fairy will not come."

Lola says, "Yes. I'll look after
      my tooth extra carefully till bedtime,
        because I really want
          my giraffe."

"When you come over tomorrow," says Lola,
"I'll have my giraffe and you can
bring your chicken..."

"... and they can be friends," says Lotta.
"Don't forget your tooth has to be
in the very, very middle of
under the pillow!"

At bedtime Lola says,
    "Charlie, I'm just going to go and
wash my tooth and make it shiny
    and clean.
        And then I...

Oh no!
My tooth!
My tooth is completely
NOT there!"

I say,
"Check again.
It must be there!"

But Lola says,
"It's completely gone,
Charlie!
My tooth is
completely
NOT
there!"

I say,
"It must be somewhere!"

So we
   start
      searching
         everywhere.

We look in the sink,

and

under
the

beds,

on the floor,

and

around the sofa.

Everywhere.

Then I have a really good idea.

"If you go to sleep and dream really
        happy dreams tonight, you will smile.
And then the tooth fairy will see
            the gap in your teeth, and she'll
    know you really did honestly
            lose your tooth!"

So Lola goes to bed.

"Dream really happy dreams.
Really happy dreams. Really happy..."

In the morning
Lola looks under the very
middle of her pillow.

She says,

"Charlie! The **tooth fairy** did come!
Look! Hurry up, Charlie,
I need to get a **giraffe!**"

When Lotta comes to play with Lola she says,
    "What is your giraffe called?"
Lola says, "He is called Giraffe.
        What is your chicken called?"
    Lotta says, "She's called Chicken! Hello, Giraffe."
    "Hello, Chicken. Oh look!
    I think they're friends," says Lola.

Lola says, "Maybe Giraffe and Chicken
would like to meet Mr Goat?"
    "But we don't have a goat," says Lotta.
"Oh no!" says Lola. "We don't have a goat!
We need more wobbly teeth!
        Have you got any more wobbly teeth?"

Lotta says, "No. Have you?"
"I don't know," says Lola. "Is this one **wobbly**?"
"No," says Lotta.
Lola says, "What about... this one?
Or this one? Or this one? Or this one..."